WALKER

The boy who can **talk** to **dogs**

Shoo began his career as an illustrator in a garden shed near Machynlleth. He drew for Michael Morpurgo and Rose Impey, but people kept encouraging him to write. Many years and more than 200 books later, Shoo has built a worldwide following for his award-winning how-to-draw videos on YouTube. http://www.shoorayner.com/

Shoo lives in the Forest of Dean with his wife and two cats.

WALKER

The boy who can **talk** to **dogs**

Shoo Rayner

Firefly

First published in 2019
by Firefly Press
25 Gabalfa Road, Llandaff North, Cardiff, CF14 2JJ
www.fireflypress.co.uk

A CIP catalogue record of this book is available from
the British Library.

ISBN 9781910080900
ebook ISBN 9781910080917

This book has been published with the support of
the Welsh Books Council.

Typeset by Elaine Sharples

Printed and bound by Pulsio, SARL

For Colum Scriven
Dog Listener

'How many more red lights?' Mum growled as she screeched the car to a halt. 'Oh no!' she groaned, glaring across the street. 'That's disgusting. Fancy letting your dog poo right there on the pavement.'

Walker looked out of the window. A poodle gazed lovingly back at him, while it did its business right in front of Poundland! The dog's owner pretended she had nothing to do with it. She held the lead behind her back and stared up to the sky as if she had a deep interest in jumbo jets. Then she pulled a pink plastic bag out of her pocket and put her hand inside it.

'At least she's taking it home.' Walker thought he really wouldn't mind having to pick up poo in a plastic bag, if *only* he could have a dog of his own. 'I wish I had a dog.'

'Oh for goodness sake!' Mum rolled her eyes. 'How many times have we been through this?'

'Millions,' Walker sighed, 'millions and trillions!'

The lights turned green and the car rolled forward. The city streets passed by, full of dogs

1

being walked on leads. He named the breeds as they passed by.

'Labrador … staffy … pug … husky … spaniel…'

Mum flicked him a glance in the rear-view mirror. She didn't have to say a word, her look said it all. Walker knew there was no point talking about it.

They were driving back from visiting Aunt Lizzie and his cousin Poppy for the day.

Poppy had rats. They weren't dogs, but at least they were pets – and they were all hers. Stinky, Scratchy, Bella and Blue whizzed around the cage doing tricks, running upside down in their wheel and squeezing through a spaghetti-like maze of plastic tubes that threaded their way up, down and across Poppy's bedroom.

'She likes you!' said Poppy, putting Bella on Walker's shoulder. The rat examined him with her pink eyes and sniffed his face, tickling his neck with her long, white, hairy whiskers. He squeezed his eyes shut and scrunched up his neck when she poked her wet little nose in his ear, as if searching for a secret stash of sunflower seeds inside. He could hear Bella's tiny breath, almost as if she was talking to him.

Back in the car, Walker remembered the feeling as he watched a large woman in a blue furry coat walk by with a tiny dog tucked under her arm. Sometimes Poppy would take Bella out for a walk in her coat pocket!

'Maybe I could have a teeny, weeny, itsy-bitsy, little chihuahua,' Walker suggested. 'They're really small. It could live in my pocket. You wouldn't even know it was there!'

Every time Walker suggested a different type of dog, praising all the virtues that the breed was well-known for, there was always the same emphatic answer:

'NO!'

A Labrador? Too bouncy!

Jack Russell? Too snappy!

Sheepdog? They need too much exercise!

Great Dane? Do you know how much they eat!?

Poodle? Old lady dogs!

Collie? Too much fur!

Fur was the problem. If Mum got too close to dogs, she suffered an allergic reaction. Her voice would go all squeaky and she would pant like a terrier that had been chasing its tail all day. She had to carry a syringe full of medicine in her handbag, just in case it got really bad. Walker didn't want to see her get ill, of course, and knew he had to think of her health first.

But he couldn't get over the idea he was *meant* to have a dog.

Walker's dad, on the other hand, just didn't like dogs. He was a quiet, gentle, cat-loving man. Lucy Lou, a plump tabby cat, curled up on his lap every night, sleeping through all the interesting TV programmes he liked to watch about history and science.

'Poor Lucy Lou!' he would say. 'Can you imagine the stress she would be put under if we had a dog in the house?'

So all Walker could do was dream of growing up and having his own place one day where he could share his life with his very own canine friend.

The city outskirts sped by. Walker flicked through the pictures of dogs on his phone and sighed deeply. Growing up seemed to be taking forever.

Mum leaned forward over the steering wheel, peered up through the windscreen and tutted. 'That man gets everywhere,' she muttered.

They were going past a huge poster of Arlington Wherewithal which read: 'You too can be as rich as me!' Arlington Wherewithal was a famous businessman, who happened to live in Foxley, the village where Walker lived with his mum and dad. Arlington's giant image stared down at them. His piercing blue eyes glittered under his wild, bushy eyebrows.

'Why's his picture up there?' Walker asked.

YOU CAN BE
AS RICH
AS ME!
THURSDAY 6th MAY

'Oh, it'll be another of his TV programmes or money-making schemes,' Mum sighed. 'People give him money so he can tell them how he got so rich. Then he gets even richer!'

Walker had known Arlington Wherewithal all his life. Not personally, like a family friend, but Arlington opened fêtes and did other things around Foxley. He made speeches and gave the prizes at Walker's school and always made sure his picture appeared in the paper. He was always on the TV too, telling everyone they could all be as rich as he was – if they just pulled their socks up!

Walker often saw Arlington walking his dogs through the village. He had two pointers. They were gun dogs, taught to fetch the birds that Arlington shot each year. In the shooting season, Foxley village reverberated to the din of Arlington's shotguns *blam-blamming* away in Foxley Woods.

Arlington lived in Foxley Manor, an enormous country mansion. He'd made a fortune from building loads of new houses on the edge of his land, making the village three times bigger than it used to be. He'd made sure they were well hidden behind Foxley Woods so he wouldn't have to see them.

Something caught Walker's eye, making him forget all about Arlington. He strained to look out of the window. The seat belt snapped tight, holding him back.

On the pavement, a woman was walking six, no, wait … seven dogs! A Labrador, Dalmatian, two sausage dogs, a Pomeranian, a West Highland terrier and a miniature bulldog. They trotted happily together on their leads, looking like a bunch of five-year-old kids on a school outing.

'She's got seven dogs!' Walker exclaimed. 'That is *so* unfair!'

'They're not hers,' Mum said, calmly.

'How do you know?'

'Look at her bag.'

A square bag dangled from the woman's shoulder. Printed on the side was a silhouette of someone walking three dogs. The message underneath read – 'Walkies! Get the app and book your dog a walk right now!'

'What does it mean?' Walker asked.

'She walks dogs for other people,' Mum explained. 'Busy people who don't have time to walk their own dogs, so they pay people to do it for them.'

'What!?' Walker's eyes popped wide open. 'You mean you can get paid for walking dogs? Well! Now I know what I want to do when I grow up! When can I leave school?'

Mum shook her head in dismay. 'Dogs! Dogs! Dogs! That's all you ever think about!'

Walker was silent for the rest of the journey home. He was thinking deep thoughts and planning a cunning plan. Maybe there was a way to sort of have a dog of his own?

Walker lay on his bed. He had cut out and stuck pictures of his favourite dogs all over the ceiling, right above his pillows. The rest of the room was filled with dog stuff – dog duvet covers, dog books, a collection of nodding dogs on the windowsill, even a dog that wagged its ears and tail when the sun was shining.

It was true, he really was a little obsessed with dogs. He knew everything about them, but could never get close to one. He was like a scientist who knows all about the moon, but has never been there.

He knew the names of all the breeds. He'd watched thousands of videos about dogs. Cute dogs, grumpy dogs, clever dogs – they were all there on the internet. Once in a while he would come across a film about dogs that had been badly treated. Some of those videos brought tears to his eyes and made him really angry. How could people do such things to those gorgeous living creatures?

He saw dogs who had been left all alone in crates, never cleaned or fed. And films about puppy farms, where puppies were bred in horrible conditions just to make money. The mothers gave birth to litter after litter until they were worn out and ill. Often the puppies died soon after they had been bought, because they had terrible diseases.

How could people be like that? And how could *they* have dogs and he couldn't, when he would so love and look after a dog of his own? If ever he saw animals being mistreated, he would do something about it. If they couldn't stand up for themselves, he would have to stand up for them instead.

He lay there, staring at the pictures, dreaming up his plan. The dog-walking lady he'd seen earlier had changed everything…

 Just at that moment, Ellie Snapchat, at Number 42 the High Street, called from her kitchen, 'Pixie! Din-dins!'

Pixie, a cheerful Border terrier, woke from a deep, sleepy dream in which she'd been chasing rabbits across white fluffy clouds. She raced down the hallway into the kitchen, skidded on the shiny wood-effect floor, crashed into the oven door, as she usually did, and rolled over three times.

Landing upright, right in front of her bowl, she wolfed down half a tin of Arlington's Chumpkin Chunks in five seconds flat. Then she raised her head and looked at Ellie as if to say, 'What's for pudding?'

 At the bottom of Number 36's garden next door, Google the Bedlington terrier leaped up and down at the fence, barking louder than a school disco.

Someone was on the other side of the fence. Google could hear them talking. They were invaders, robbers, ne'er-do-wells! Google knew his job was to protect his master's castle. They might be cut-throats or axe-murderers!

Google raced up the garden and barked at the patio doors, but no one took any notice. He barked at the barbecue under its green cover. He barked at the toy car, that had been abandoned upside down on the path like a miniature road traffic accident. Then he tore back to the bottom of the garden, jumping up and down, up and down, scratching the wooden fence panel, barking, barking, barking!

Arlington Wherewithal's head appeared above the fence panel. His fierce, cold, blue eyes stared down.

Google froze and stared back. They looked at each other for a few, long, silent seconds.

Arlington jerked his head and said, 'BOO!'

Google was so surprised, he put his tail between his legs, ran up the garden and hid under the barbecue covers, where he stayed, shaking and whimpering, until he could hear that the nasty man had gone, his cruel laughter fading away.

In Number 34, the house that didn't look like any of the others in the row, Jenny Little hid behind the curtains in her sitting room and peered out of the window.

Arlington Wherewithal was having an animated discussion with another man on the other side of her garden fence. He pointed right at her house, then at a map. Jenny knew they were up to no good.

The other man took pictures of Jenny's house and garden on his phone. He snapped photographs of her leafy vegetable plot, her colourful flower garden and the dear little greenhouse where her juicy tomatoes were growing nicely. He filmed the small round pond with its tiny waterfall, where her fish swam lazily by, waiting for her to feed them.

The man pointed towards her fruit-laden apple trees. Jenny could hear them. They spoke in loud, bossy voices as if they owned the place. The man said, 'They'll need chopping down!'

Jenny's dog growled.

'Come away from the window, Stella,' Jenny hissed. 'Don't let them see you.'

Number 34 the High Street was one of the few houses that Arlington Wherewithal had not built. It was one of the old, village houses, built long, long before Arlington moved to Foxley Manor.

The new houses had been made to *look* like they were old, but they'd been built close together, with smaller gardens and just enough room to park a car down the side of the house.

Number 34, or Hazeldean as it used to be called, was different. Hazeldean was a detached, wooden house standing in its own large garden, which Jenny loved and tended, making a haven for insects, birds and butterflies. Jenny made jams and jellies from the fruit and scented bags and potpourri from the flowers in her large flower beds.

Arlington Wherewithal wanted her house. He had always wanted her house. There was nothing else in the world he wanted as much. Arlington was used to getting his own way. He thought money could buy *anything*.

So he made Jenny an offer that he thought she could not refuse. He offered her so much money for her house and the land that anyone else would have said, 'Thank you very much!' and gone off on a world cruise to celebrate.

But not Jenny. Her great-grandfather had built the house with his bare hands, way back in the old days when it was common land and the law in the village said that if you could clear a piece of land, build a chimney, light a fire and get smoke coming from the top, within twenty-four hours, the land was yours to live on forever.

That's what great-grandfather Little had done. He cleared what was now Jenny's garden and built a chimney in twenty-four hours. He built the rest of the house around the chimney in his own time. He dug the foundations by hand, sawed all the timber and nailed every plank and hammered on every roof tile.

The house was special. Very few houses from those days survived. One day, someone realised how rare Jenny's house was. An historic building preservation order was made to protect it, so no one could knock it down. Jenny had all the legal papers to say it was hers and hers alone. They even made a TV programme about Hazeldean.

Number 34 was not for sale.

But Arlington was not a man to take no for an answer. When he wasn't smiling at a camera or giving prizes at the village fête, Arlington was a bully. A mean, brutish, conniving, tricky, deceitful bully.

Jenny sank into her armchair and peeped through the gap in the curtains again. 'He's up to something, Stella,' she said. 'Arlington's got a new plan and I really don't think I've got the strength to fight him anymore.'

Stella put her head in Jenny's lap and looked up with big, brown, trusting eyes.

Jenny smiled and scratched Stella's golden fur behind the ears. 'Sometimes,' she whispered, 'I think you understand every word I say.'

'Can I put this card up in your window, Mr Bonus?' Walker asked.

Mr Bonus brushed his thick moustache, picked up the card Walker had placed on the shop counter and read it aloud in a strong Lithuanian accent.

Mr Bonus read it again. 'I don't understand. Explain, please.'

Walker told him that he was setting up a dog walking business. People would pay him to walk their dogs.

Mr Bonus looked confused. 'Why they pay you to walk dogs? My dog, Boss, he's happy in back yard keeping out the bad men. He don't need walking.'

Walker explained that most people liked to take their dogs for a walk every day, but some were too busy, so they would pay him to walk them.

'Hmm!' Mr Bonus gave an appreciative nod. 'That's crazy, but that's *good* business. For notice card in my window, I charge one pound for two weeks.'

'Oh!' Walker was crestfallen. He picked up his card and looked at it wistfully. He hadn't thought he might have to pay to put it in the shop window. His business was going to fail at the first step.

He'd worked so hard on the card too. He'd drawn a great stick-man picture of a responsible-looking person walking a stick-dog that was carrying a stick in its mouth – he really liked that little joke. He'd added his home phone number and address and printed some smaller copies on the computer, so he could give them to people walking their dogs.

Walker was particularly proud of 'Competitive Rates'. He'd seen the phrase on other adverts, it sounded very professional. He had no idea how much people would be willing to pay him.

Mr Bonus smiled. 'I like this. I like to see young person be entrepreneur – be businessman. I make you business offer. I put card in shop window for free. You get business … then you pay me!' Mr Bonus spat on his hand and held it out across the counter. 'Deal?'

Walker thought for a moment, smiled, spat in his palm and shook Mr Bonus's hand firmly. 'Deal!' he laughed.

Outside the shop, Walker watched Mr Bonus pin the card to the board in the window. He smiled to himself. He was in business! Soon he would have as many dogs as he could cope with – even if they were part-time.

Through the shop's wrought-iron side gate, Boss, the shop's Alsatian guard dog, watched Walker pass along the pavement. Then he dropped his head and continued pacing up and down the back yard.

Boss was so bored. When he wasn't pacing up and down, up and down, he lay in his kennel and

l of the day a real bad man might climb
e wall so that he could sink his teeth into
g, bad bottom!

 The next day, Mum and Walker
popped into the shop on the way
home from school. Anje, Mr
Bonus's daughter, was behind the
counter in her school uniform.
She went to Walker's school.

'Hey,' Anje laughed. 'Got any customers yet?'

'What's this?' Mum asked, confused.

Walker knew he should have let his parents
know about his plans, but he just sort of forgot.
'I've started a dog-walking business,' he said,
looking down and talking to his shoes. 'Mr Bonus
let me put a card in the shop window.'

'Oh, Walker!' Mum sighed loudly. 'You can't
just start up a business at your age. I mean, surely
you need a licence or training or something?'

'Is a good thing!' said Mr Bonus, lurching out
of the storeroom at the back of the shop, weighed
down by a giant box of toilet rolls. 'Is good for
Walker to be businessman.'

'But I'm a local councillor,' Mum protested. 'I have to uphold the law!'

'Is no law!' Mr Bonus laughed. 'He just a boy. No worries about licence – no one cares about licence for boy – it's pocket for money. It's big initiative.' Mr Bonus put an arm round Walker and patted him on the head. 'He's a good boy. You should be proud!'

Anje winked at Walker.

Mum tut-tutted and shook her head all the way home.

A folded piece of paper sat waiting for them on the doormat. Walker's name was written on the outside in wobbly biro. Inside was a wobbly biro message:

Hazeldean
34 The High St.
Foxley

Dear Mr Walker,
please would you
walk my dog, Stella?
Please call anytime
Jenny Little

It was signed Jenny Little and the address was Hazeldean – Number 34, the High Street.

'That's the lady in the house with the pretty garden,' said Mum. 'That's okay, I don't mind you helping her. I don't think she can walk very far. She could do with someone to help walk her dog.'

'Does that mean I can go and see her about it?' Walker asked. He put his sweetest face on. The one that Mum could never say no to. 'Can I?'

'Oh, alright, but come straight back and tell me what you've agreed.'

At that exact same moment, Mr and Mrs Sowerby in Chestnut Avenue stood at their open front door, waggling a dog lead, enthusiastically calling inside the house, 'Come on, Khan … walkies!'

Khan, an old, tired chow, padded into the hallway from his bed in the study. His tired, hooded, old eyes observed the smiling couple trying to chivvy him along. His tired, old ears only heard bits of what they were saying.

Khan took one look at the lead, turned around, padded back to his bed and collapsed in a heap of fur and snuffled complaints. The Sowerbys gently closed the front door, gave each other a meaningful look and followed Khan to the study. They patted the old dog on the head and stroked his thick, thick fur.

'Oh, Khan,' they sighed. 'What are we going to do with you?'

Khan snorted, laid his head on his paws and closed his eyes. He was old and tired. He couldn't be bothered going for walkies anymore.

He snuffled and growled, dreaming that he was his young self again, remembering how he would run about Foxley Fields, barking his head off, letting all the other dogs know who was in charge! He wasn't ready to give up. There was a little bit of life in the old dog yet.

'Hello,' said Walker. 'I'm Walker.'

The lady who'd answered the door looked a little confused.

'I'm … the dog walker?' Walker reassured her. 'You left a message at our house?'

Jenny Little looked surprised. 'Oh! I was expecting someone a bit older. The drawing in the shop window looked like an … adult.'

Stella bounced out of the door and jumped up onto Walker's legs.

'Stella!' Jenny scolded. 'That's very naughty!'

'I don't mind,' Walker laughed. 'She's lovely!'

Stella licked Walker's face, made excited doggy noises, and thumped her waggy tail against the door frame.

'She likes you!' Jenny smiled. 'You'd better come in.'

Walker told Jenny all about himself and his new business, while Jenny made a pot of tea. 'Would you like some cake?' she asked, showing him a gorgeous, plump Victoria sponge. 'It's home-made?'

He told her about his mum's dog allergy, how

he had always wanted to have a dog and why he'd started a dog-walking business. 'It's the best of both worlds,' he explained. 'I get to be with dogs but without my family being involved.'

After two slices of cake, Walker and Jenny were like old friends. Walker sat on the sofa with Stella next to him. She let him stroke her long, soft, fluffy ears while she looked up at him with adoring eyes.

'Well, you certainly have a way with dogs,' Jenny laughed. 'She's putty in your hands! I'd be happy to let you take her out for walks. I can't walk very far anymore and she really needs a good run every day. How much do you charge? I'm not rich, I can't pay you much.'

'I'd walk Stella for free,' Walker said immediately. 'It's not about the money. I just want to be with dogs.'

'Well, that really is a competitive rate!' laughed Jenny. 'But that wouldn't be fair. Maybe you could walk Stella after school every day and at the weekends. Would ten pounds each week be enough?'

Ten pounds – he'd be rich in no time! He was about to spit on his hand, like Mr Bonus had, but thought that maybe that was a bit too Lithuanian for Jenny. 'It's a deal!' he said.

Stella sighed contentedly and rested her head in Walker's lap.

'Can you start tomorrow?' Jenny asked.

'I'd start today,' said Walker, 'but Mum says I have to go home and tell her what we've agreed first.'

Jenny nodded. 'That's very sensible. Good! I'll see you tomorrow after school.'

Walker pedalled like a maniac all the way home. He was so excited. Stella was gorgeous.

He and Mum agreed that he'd come home and get changed after school before he went dog walking. He'd have special dog clothes, which he would always have to change in and out of in the garage before he came into the house. Then he'd have to wash his hands with antibacterial soap. He had to be careful to protect his mum from dog hair.

'I'm putting my injection thing here on the hall table so we all know where it is,' she told Walker and Dad after supper. 'Just in case!'

Lucy Lou's nose twitched. As Walker bent down to stroke her, she smelled the dog on him. Her fur frizzed up, making her look like a giant, round furball. She leaped up the stairs and sat shivering on the fifth step from the top, mewing like a pathetic little kitten.

'You've upset her,' Dad whined. 'Must you do this dog-walking thing? Lucy Lou hates dogs.' He picked up his little darling, took her to the sitting room and settled down for the night, watching a programme about volcanoes on the geography channel.

Nothing was going to stop Walker. No one was going to thwart his plans. He could barely sleep that night. At school the next day, he scarcely heard a word that Miss Coleshaw said in class. All he could think about was Stella. The hands on the class clock went round so-o-o-o-o sl-o-o-o-o-wly!

At the school gate, Mum wouldn't stop talking rubbish about what Skylar's mum had said to Macey's mum about Daniel's mum, who was going away *again* on another expensive holiday, leaving Daniel with his grandparents… Walker liked Daniel and felt sorry for him, but Stella was waiting for him.

He sighed loudly and kept walking off purposefully, hoping Mum would follow him home. Eventually she did.

Walker changed into his dog-walking clothes, got on his bike, snuck down Lime Passage, crossed the High Street at the crossing, rode down the pavement, unlatched the gate at Number 34 and leaned his bike up against the front porch.

He didn't need to ring the doorbell. Stella came bounding around the side of the house, bouncing like a spring lamb. Jenny appeared behind her.

'I thought it must be you,' she said. 'Stella has been in such an excitable mood today, it's like she knew you were coming!'

Jenny suggested he could go out of the gate at the bottom of the garden and through the trees to Foxley Field where, if he felt confident, he could let Stella off the lead for a run about.

'You'll need these too,' she said, handing Walker some thin plastic bags. 'It's the worst bit of dog-walking, but you'll soon get used to it. There's a dog-poo bin by the gate near the church. You can drop it there.'

Walker stared at the plastic bags. They were green and silky to the touch. He'd looked up lots about dog-walking on line and this was the bit he wasn't really looking forward to.

'Have fun,' Jenny called, as they disappeared into the trees. She smiled and shook her head. She wasn't sure which of the two would have the most fun … Walker or Stella!

The gate closed behind them with a click. Walker stepped out alone – with a dog – on his own – with Stella.

All his life, Walker had dreamed of this day.

Leaves rustled in the warm spring breeze. Birds twittered on the branches. Blue sky shone in patches through the tree canopy above him. Midges danced in shafts of sunlight that streamed down through the trees, dappling the bluebells. He savoured every tiny detail so he would never forget. The heady perfume of the bluebells stamped the moment on his memory forever.

He'd always imagined there would be a magic sort of electricity flowing through the lead between him and a dog. But now he was here … the lead was just an old bit of leather, limp in his hand.

He felt a different sort of magic though: excitement and trepidation at the same time. A tiny power source was beating, pulsing deep inside him. It was something to do with being on his own, in charge, trusted and responsible. But it was also being alone with Stella, connected to her by invisible threads of … what?

Stella picked a stick up in her mouth and trotted along beside him, happy and content.

Every now and then, she'd drag him over to a tree so she could sniff the smells left by other dogs. Then she would wee! Walker watched her from the corner of his eye, to see if there was a poo that needed cleaning up … not yet! It was amazing how many times she could wee though!

The strip of woods behind Jenny's house opened up into Foxley Fields. Walker had known it all his life. His family had picnicked there, flown kites and gone sledging down the hill at the far end if it snowed.

Foxley Fields and the village green were the two places where villagers came to play and be together. The village fête was held here at the end of the summer holidays. Cakes, flowers and vegetables were shown and judged on the green. The fête sports and dog show were held across the road, behind the church.

Dog show? Walker wondered if … maybe?

Stella dropped the stick at his feet and gave him a hopeful look.

'Do you want me to throw it for you?'

Stella crouched and wagged her tail.

'Okay, I'm going to let you off the lead, Stella. Promise you'll come back when I call you?'

Stella made an excited, whiny, whistly noise that seemed to say yes, so Walker unclipped the lead and let her run free.

He threw the stick high into the air. 'Go fetch, girl!' he laughed out loud. He felt set free himself.

Stella chased after the stick, never taking her eyes off it. The stick bounced and she caught it clean.

'Well done!' Walker called to her. 'Now bring it back!'

She bounded back, slowed to a trot, circled round behind him and dropped the stick at his feet. She sat, panting and dribbling, waiting for Walker to throw it again.

And that's how they played for the next half hour, throwing, catching, running and jumping, until something caught Stella's eye … a rabbit!

Rabbits were the one thing she couldn't resist. The sight of one made her forget everything. She was off like a rocket!

'Stella! Come back!' Walker took off after her, crashing through a screen of low-hanging oak leaves into the darker woods at the top of the hill.

He followed the sound of her barking. Dark, twisted, gnarly tree trunks surrounded him. The thin path led around a rocky outcrop. The last thing Walker expected, as he turned the corner, was to hear a man's deep voice.

'You! Boy! What d'you think you're doing on my land?'

Anje, Mr Bonus's daughter, stepped out into the sunshine of the yard at the back of the shop. She'd been ripping open cardboard boxes full of tins and putting the price stickers on beans and spaghetti hoops, then filling up any empty shelves in the shop. She sat down on the old bench with her cup of tea and let the sun warm her face.

Boss padded over and sat down beside her. He loved Anje. He'd known her as long as he could remember. When she was little, she rode on his back like he was a pony.

'Oh Boss,' she sighed, putting her arms around the big dog's neck, burying her face into his fur. Sometimes she wished that she could just have a bit of time on her own to do her own thing.

The shop never stopped. There was always some job or other, opening boxes, stacking shelves, folding empty boxes, taking out the rubbish, smiling at the customers. She'd known how to operate the cash till since she was eight. When she wasn't doing all that, she had to help with the cooking *and* do her homework!

Anje drained her tea, picked up the brush and pan by the back door, scooped up Boss's poos that were dotted around the yard and, holding her breath and wrinkling her nose, dropped them into the poo bin. She gave Boss one last hug and went back to stacking soap powder.

 'Well, Boy! Has the cat got your tongue?' Arlington Wherewithal and his gamekeeper, Osmo, blocked the path. They both carried shotguns crooked under their arms. The guns were broken open, ready for loading. They were safe, but intimidating. Walker had never seen a gun in real life before and he felt very nervous.

'I-I-I'm walking my dog,' he stammered.

'I see no dog!' Arlington boomed, in a theatrical sort of way, looking all around him in an exaggerated manner. He laughed at his little joke and Osmo bared his teeth in a sort of grin.

Just then, Stella bounded towards them. When she saw the two men, she screeched to a halt and cowered behind Walker.

Arlington narrowed his eyes. 'That's not your dog! That's Mrs Little's dog.'

'Miss,' said Walker.

'What?' Arlington wasn't used to boys answering back. Arlington wasn't used to boys at all.

'Er ... it's *Miss* Little,' Walker corrected. 'She's not Mrs. I'm walking her dog for her. I've started a dog-walking business.'

Walker pulled one of his small adverts out of his pocket and showed it to Arlington, who examined it closely. An insincere smile crept across his unnaturally suntanned face, like a fungus spreading across a rotten orange.

'Walker the dog walker!' he said in a slow, drawn-out, meaningful way. 'Is Walker your name?'

'Yes, sir.'

'Ha!' he said at last. 'That's most enterprising! I like to see a boy setting up in business and making some money. Reminds me of myself when I was young. I was breeding dogs by the time I was twelve and started my dog food company when I was sixteen. I was a millionaire before I was twenty-one, y'know? Good for you! Now, get off my land!'

Arlington made a strange high-pitched whistle through his teeth. Seconds later, his two pointers bounded up the path behind him. They stood to attention either side of their master and stared menacingly at Walker and Stella. Stella whimpered. Walker had read enough dog books and seen enough training videos to know not to stare back at them. His eyes drifted upwards until they met Arlington's cold, dazzling blue gaze.

'Come on, Stella, let's go.' Walker clipped the lead onto Stella's collar and turned to take her home. 'Sorry, sir. We won't come here again.'

He could feel Arlington's frosty stare boring into his back. He only felt safe again when they broke through the edge of the trees and felt the freeing sunshine of Foxley Fields shine down on them.

'I need a poo!' said Stella.

For a moment, Walker thought that he'd just heard Stella say that she needed a poo. He stared at her and frowned. Had Arlington Wherewithal freaked him out so much he'd started hearing things?

Stella was busy. She stared at him in a cross-eyed sort of way. She was doing a poo on the grass! She bounced up, turned around and sniffed her work.

'You'd better bag that up,' she said.

Walker let his mouth hang wide open in astonishment! 'Stella! You can talk!'

Stella tilted her head. 'Well, of course,' she said. 'All dogs can talk.'

'But…' Walker was lost for words.

She took a deep breath. 'All dogs can talk,' she repeated. 'It's just that not many humans can understand.'

'But…' Walker was still lost for words.

'You must be what humans call a dog whisperer. It's a stupid name. You're not whispering at all, you're talking quite normally. You can talk to dogs and dogs can talk to you.'

'But…' Walker was so confused.

'I've never met one, before,' Stella continued, 'but I've heard about them. Pixie at Number 42 went to a dog whisperer once. She said he was very nice and he convinced her to stop chewing shoes and slippers.'

Walker found his voice again. 'How did he do that?'

She snuffled a laugh. 'He told her she might catch verrucas on the end of her nose and would end up looking like a stick of broccoli!'

He laughed. 'So, you mean we can talk to each other?'

'Isn't that what we are doing now?'

Walker had a million questions to ask, but didn't know where to begin. 'What about Miss Little, I mean Jenny, can she talk to you?'

'Of course not!' Stella shook her head violently. She'd got leaves in her ears while chasing the rabbit. 'Dog whisperers are very rare, you know? Jenny is so sweet, I couldn't hope to live with anyone kinder. I understand a bit of what she says, but not like I can understand you. It's hard to explain. Sometimes I don't understand her at all, which usually means I've done something naughty – which reminds me!'

Stella tilted her head towards the poo, as if to say, 'Haven't you forgotten something?'

Walker pulled out a plastic bag. He put his hand inside the bag like a glove. He took a deep breath, reached down and put the bag over the poo and scraped it up off the grass.

He tried not to think about it. About how it was still warm, how it was softish to the touch, how only a thin skin of biodegradable plastic stood between him and this little pile of dog poo. He turned the bag inside out and tied it up as tight as he knew how.

'Sorry,' said Stella, as she watched Walker deposit the bag in the bin by the church gate. 'I hate that man, Arlington. Jenny is so scared of him. Being so close to him in the woods back there, I just couldn't hold it in!'

Walker thought of the ice-blue eyes that had made him feel so uneasy. 'He is very bossy. He acts like he owns the place!'

'That's the problem,' Stella laughed. 'He does!'

They arrived at the back gate of Number 36.

'Why didn't you speak to me before?' Walker asked.

'I don't know, I suppose it seemed a bit odd

talking to a human. But now I feel like I've always known you. As for that man Arlington... I just couldn't stay silent any longer.'

'It does feel a bit strange talking to you,' Walker admitted, 'but it also seems so natural, like you're a friend.'

'There you are!' Jenny called across from her vegetable patch, where she was thinning out seedlings and weeding.

Stella seemed to switch off and became a dog again. She winked at Walker, barked and ran to Jenny, bouncing around her, greeting her with little woofs, snuffles and licks, just like any other dog would.

'She looks like she's had a really good time. Thank you so much. Say thank you for my walk, Stella.'

Stella woofed, ran back to Walker and jumped up for him to make a fuss.

'She really likes you!' Jenny smiled. 'See you again tomorrow?'

'I can't wait!' said Walker. There were so many questions he wanted to ask his new canine friend.

 Every day, after school, Walker got changed as quickly as possible, getting ready to take Stella for a walk. She was always waiting for him, bouncing up and down with excitement.

'She knows when you're coming!' Jenny said. 'About five minutes ago, she went and picked up her lead. She's been carrying it around ever since, waiting for you to arrive!'

When she was with Jenny and other people, Stella acted like any other dog. But when they were alone, Walker and Stella were just two friends, out for a walk together.

Every day Walker threw sticks, or an old tennis ball, until they were both worn out, he from throwing and Stella from fetching, then they'd sit at the top of the hill, away from passers-by, and talk about what it was like to be a dog or a human. There were some things that humans did that Stella just couldn't understand.

'Why do people go to work?' she wanted to know. Some of her friends were left alone all day, locked up like prisoners. At least Jenny was with her all day and let her out into the garden with her, even if she couldn't take her out for walks anymore.

Walker was fascinated by Stella's sense of smell. Stella could smell a lamp post or a tree and know exactly who had been there before and when. More than that, she could tell if the dog leaving the smell was unwell. She could even tell their breed and what size they were – all by smelling their wee!

One afternoon, while out walking with Stella, Walker was desperate for a wee himself, so he went behind a large oak tree where no one could see him. Stella had a good long sniff. 'Mmm! That's a very friendly smell,' she said. 'Did you have fish for lunch?'

'We had fish fingers at school.'

'And peas?'

'That's amazing!' Walker laughed.

Anyone watching would have just seen a boy talking to his dog, the way that boys do. They would not have heard his dog talking back.

It's a strange language that dog whisperers speak. It's almost like the words they say have another meaning that only dogs can understand. It works the other way around too. All the yaps and barks and squeaks and growls have quite another meaning that only make sense to the special, chosen few, like Walker.

Stella often talked about Arlington Wherewithal. She didn't know why, but she knew that Jenny was frightened of him and that made Stella frightened of him too.

'Sometimes,' she said, 'the wind blows across from his house, and I think I hear the sound of dogs and puppies crying – maybe I'm just imagining it. But I do not like that man. I don't think there's a dog in the village that does.'

'Ten pounds a week!' Walker's dad looked astounded. 'Why, that's over five hundred pounds a year!'

Walker was feeling rich and successful, holding up the ten-pound note that Jenny had given him.

'That's a lot of money,' said Mum. 'You should open a savings account and not spend it all.'

'I really want to buy something for Stella,' said Walker, 'and I need to pay Mr Bonus for the card in his window.'

'Oh well, if you're going to the shop...' Mum checked in the fridge. 'Can you get some milk while you are there?'

It was Saturday morning. Anje was in charge behind the counter. She looked different out of school uniform. Her long hair was plaited round the top of her head and she wore an old-fashioned denim jacket with badges sewn all over it.

'Hey, Walker. How are you doing?' Anje smiled. She didn't smile much at school. Sometimes it was easy to forget she was there, at the back of the class, working away quietly. But when she did smile … there was something about the way she wrinkled up her nose, and the sun had brought out her freckles, painting little brown flecks across her nose that made her look…

'I-I'm good,' Walker spluttered. 'I-Is your dad here?'

Anje shook her head. 'He's gone to the cash and carry to get more stuff. Can I help?'

'No, I just came to get some milk,' he said, picking up a bottle of semi-skimmed. He mooched around the rest of the shop. The pet food corner was full of Arlington's Chumpkin Chunks.

Walker examined the few pet toys on display. There was nothing special – just knobbly, rubber bones with bells in them, or dried-up, leathery chewy toys and something squeaky that a dog would destroy within five minutes.

He'd just finished paying for the milk, when Mr Bonus bustled through the door. Walker perked up. He took a pound coin out of his pocket and placed it proudly on the counter. 'That's the pound I owe for my card.'

Mr Bonus smiled and nudged Anje. 'This is good boy! He's good businessman!' He turned to Walker. 'Hey, you want to leave card up for two more weeks?'

Walker shook his head. 'I don't think I could cope with more than one dog at the moment, but thank you.'

Mr Bonus slapped his forehead. 'Hey! Wait till you see what I got!' He went off to his van and was soon back with more stuff.

'You give me idea. If stupid people pay you to walk their dogs, they gonna want one of these too.' He placed a box on the table and cut along the printed dotted lines, then he opened it up to make a display. Inside were balls on sticks, wrapped up in plastic.

'This is good!' said Mr Bonus, handing one to

Walker. 'Make you throw ball very far. Make dog do all the running. You take it easy!'

Anje picked one out of the box and looked at it. 'Can I have one for Boss?' she asked.

Mr Bonus furrowed his eyebrows. 'Boss is guard dog, he not need exercise! Ha! You think I going to pay some dog walkie person to throw balls for Boss? Ha! Ha! Ha!' Mr Bonus laughed till tiny tears squeezed out of the corner of his eyes.

Anje sighed and tidied up the till receipts.

The ball-thrower was the perfect present for Stella. 'I'd like to buy one, please.' Walker had money in his pocket now, and was in the mood to spend it. 'How much are they?'

Mr Bonus patted Walker on the shoulder. 'Don't worry,' he winked. 'I give you a good price!'

 Boss was waiting by the wrought-iron gate as Walker passed by. Boss caught his eye, tilted his head and raised an eyebrow a millimetre. Walker replied with a similar motion and a nod of acknowledgement. They couldn't have a conversation right there on the street, but Boss knew that he knew that they could if they wanted to.

It all happened in a micro second. Any humans watching would never have noticed the exchange – unless they were a dog whisperer too.

 The day of the Village Fête was as crazy as always. Over the past few days, tents and marquees had gone up on the village green. Colourful triangular bunting was strung between the lamp

posts and cars were parked all over the place. Tiny fairground rides were set up for the little children and there were coconut shies and tombola stalls down by the pond.

Walker offered to help Jenny carry all her entries over to the judging tents. She was entering something in almost every category. Peas, beans, onions, carrots, tomatoes, an enormous marrow that Walker had to take over the road in a wheelbarrow because it was so heavy, and flowers of every description. He looked like a walking flower shop!

Then there were the cakes and biscuits. Walker knew how good they were! He'd been walking Stella every day during the long, summer holiday. With no school, Walker and Stella spent most afternoons together. He would often offer to help Jenny with little jobs around the place, just so he could spend a bit longer with Stella. Every time they returned from a walk, exhausted from throwing and chasing balls and sticks, there was always a slice of cake waiting for him and they were all delicious!

'Can I take Stella to the dog show in Foxley Fields?' he asked her, placing a stack of cake tins on one of the long, wooden trestle tables in the tent.

'Why, yes, of course!' said Jenny. 'She'd love it. She's so good with you, I'm sure she'd behave herself.'

Walker looked down at Stella, and winked. 'She'll be a champion!' he smiled.

 Foxley Fields, which was usually so empty when Walker walked Stella, was packed with people and dogs. The little kids were running egg-and-spoon races,

concentrating fiercely on their spoons. Some were actually holding their eggs on the spoons with a finger. 'That's cheating!' Walker laughed to himself.

Running lanes had been painted on the grass in white chalk. Proud parents, brothers, sisters, uncles, aunts and grandparents spilled onto the racing track, screaming at the top of their voices. 'Pick the egg up, Poppet. Keep going... No! The other way!'

The parents competed in the sack race, hop-hop-hopping along like demented Duracell bunnies, getting hotter and redder, until they collapsed over the finishing line in fits of giggles as their children jumped on top of them. Tug-of-war teams from the five surrounding villages limbered up – the tug-of-war was serious business!

The dog show ring was a large rectangle marked out by ropes, tied to stakes in the ground. Walker had never been to this part of the fête before. Because his mum wanted to keep as far away from dogs as possible, he'd only ever been to the cakes and flowers contests on the village green.

But this year was different. Now that he had Stella, his parents felt a lot more confident about letting him walk around the village on his own.

'What do we do?' Stella asked.

'I don't know.' Walker didn't want anyone to see him and Stella talking, so he tried speak without moving his lips, while looking in the opposite direction. He looked like a bad ventriloquist. 'I think we have to go there first.' He nodded at a sign.

A man and a woman sat behind a table at the entrance to the ring. They watched Walker and Stella approach.

'Hello!' the woman smiled. She leaned over the table and took a look at Stella. 'Who have we got here, then? Are you entering the show?'

'This is Stella,' said Walker. 'We don't know what to do.'

'It's very simple,' said the man. 'You need to choose which category you want to compete in...' He leaned over the table to look at Stella. 'I would put her in for the prettiest girl competition.' He smiled. 'She's bound to win that! When you hear your name called, go into the ring with the others and line up. The judge is Mr Arlington Wherewithal. We're so lucky to have him. He's very important in the dog-judging world.'

Stella growled and pulled away from the table, straining to drag Walker away.

'I'll be back in a minute!' Walker chuckled nervously.

'Ha-ha! Don't put her in for the obedience category!' the woman laughed.

'I'm not going near that man!' Stella hissed. 'I don't want *him* touching me! And I'm not going to enter the prettiest girl category either! That's so sexist!'

Walker didn't feel too comfortable about meeting Arlington either, not after seeing him in the woods. They headed back to the table.

'It's okay,' Walker told the couple. 'We'll just watch so we know what to do next time.'

'Are you sure?' asked the man. 'It's free for kids, and there are prizes too.'

'I'm just looking after her,' Walker said, as if that explained everything.

There were stalls around the show ring, selling all sorts of doggy stuff. There were artists selling drawings of dogs and other pets. Another stall was heaving with plates and china stuff with pictures of dogs on. The dogs' home charity had a table full of cards, badges and stickers.

As the dog show got underway, an old man sitting on a straw bale shifted over to let Walker sit down. 'She's a pretty one,' the old man said, letting Stella sniff his hand before he stroked the top of her head. 'Are you showing her?'

'No,' said Walker, trying to think up a reason why. 'She's not been well.'

The old man nodded. 'Well, you're looking bonny now!' he told Stella in a *who's a good doggy* sort of voice.

The lady from the table entered the ring holding a megaphone. 'First of all, ladies and gentlemen...' she announce in her tinny, electronic voice, '...will you please put your hands together for our esteemed judge, Mr Arlington Wherewithal!'

The crowd cheered and clapped as Arlington strode into the ring. He raised his bowler hat in greeting, to acknowledge the praise of the onlookers. Various enamel judging badges adorned the lapel of his white coat, that flapped open over his tweed jacket, red trousers and fancy leather boots.

When Arlington came to examine the animals, the naughty dogs suddenly stood to attention, letting him poke and prod and feel for bits of fat that shouldn't be there.

Stella shivered at the thought of being manhandled by *that* man!

The old man next to Walker watched the proceedings with his chin resting on his walking stick. He leaned towards Walker. 'Arlington is so good with the dogs,' he said. His face cracked into a smile. He pointed with his stick. 'Look how they respond to him. He has them completely under his control.'

'That's because they're terrified of him,' Stella whispered.

Arlington scratched his head and stroked his chin. He put his hands on his hips and looked at all the dogs again. In the end, he chose a fluffy white bichon frise and handed a rosette to the happy owner, a girl in the class below Walker at school. Her parents proudly took photographs of Arlington shaking her hand and shaking the dog's paw.

'Your dog is much prettier!' the old man told Walker. 'You should have been in there, you know? She'd have won it easily!'

Stella growled and tugged her lead to pull Walker away. 'What's with all this pretty business?' she whispered to Walker.

'There's a handsome boy category too,' said Walker.

'Oh!' Stella snorted and rolled her eyes. 'I suppose that makes it all right then!' Her eyes darted about the field taking in all the activity. 'What's going on over there?'

 At that same moment, Anje took five minutes out for a cup of tea with Boss in the back yard. The day of the Village Fête was always busy in the shop.

The shop was right in between the green and Foxley Fields, so she could hear all the fun, music and laughter going on around her. But she was stuck behind the counter, selling ice creams and cups of coffee from their new automatic coffee machine.

She drained her glass of water, ruffled Boss between the ears and went back in the shop to re-stock the freezer with Magnums and ice lollies.

 At the top of Foxley Fields, four young men were lifting up the front of an old car, while another was pushing a bale of straw underneath it. When the car was resting on the straw bale, they began unbolting one of the wheels.

There was a lot of joking and laughter between them. One of them bolted on a new wheel. It had no tyre, it was just the metal rim. The others focussed on different jobs. They all knew what to do.

One ran a long, thin piece of rope to the end of the field, then he tied something to the end of it.

It looked like a stuffed, tartan, sausage-shaped bag with long floppy ears. Another of the team tied the other end of the rope to the wheel drum on the car. At the same time, the others built a sort of wall out of straw bales, leaving a gap in the middle for the rope to run through.

One lad got into the driving seat and started the engine. He leaned out of the window and called down the hill, 'Ready, Mikey?'

Mikey raised an arm and gave the thumbs up sign. 'Ready, Conn!'

Conn revved the car engine and the drum began to turn, winding in the rope, so that the sausage at the other end streaked up the field, with its ears flapping crazily.

'Rabbit!' Stella yelped. She was off so fast that she pulled the lead clean out of Walker's hand.

Walker took off in pursuit. 'Stella! Come back!'

Stella tore after the sausage, which disappeared through the hole in the wall of straw bales. 'Where'd it go?' she panted, poking her nose into the square straw tunnel. 'I saw it go this way!'

'Stella!' Walker panted, as he caught up with her. 'It's not real. It's just a thing on a piece of rope.' He caught her lead and walked her round behind the straw wall, to show her how it worked.

The young men were in fits of laughter. 'She's fast!' said Conn, the driver of the car. 'You should let her compete.'

Walker looked confused.

'Drag racing,' he explained. 'We put a load of dogs at the bottom of the field and they all chase the rabbit.

First one to the wall is the winner.'

'Yeah! Yeah!' Stella barked. 'I wanna do it! I wanna do it! That sounds like so much fun.'

'We have a final race where any size or shape of

dog can join in,' another of the young men said. 'That's amazing fun. The little ones go crazy for it!'

'You don't have a prettiest girl category, do you?' Walker asked.

Conn laughed. 'Don't be daft! Just big, medium and small pets and big and little working dogs. She'd be medium. She's fast – she's a winner, I reckon. See you later?'

Walker looked at Stella. Her eyes shone and her tongue was falling out of the side of her mouth as she panted to get her breath back.

'Nothing would stop her!' Walker smiled. 'Come on, girl. Let's get you a drink.'

Khan walked into the ring and stood to attention. He knew what to do.

He'd known it was the fête this weekend. The signs had been there all week. Mrs Sowerby had been baking cakes and Mr Sowerby had been preparing him for the show, brushing Khan's thick fur, talking to him in those irritating baby voices. 'Does Khany-wany want to come to the show this year?'

It was the one day in the year he could be bothered to get up and go out.

He'd been entered into the old-timer's category. That was embarrassing, but at least he didn't have to do anything like the agility dogs did, leaping over fences and disappearing down tunnels. He just had to stand there and look proud. Khan was good at that.

Arlington Wherewithal strode up and down, arms folded, assessing the qualities of all the dogs – staring them out. One by one, the dogs dropped to the ground and lay on the grass. Caramelina, a tall, willowy Afghan that Khan had known all his life, actually rolled over, closed her eyes and went to sleep.

'It's last dog standing,' Khan told himself. He'd been to the show every year since he was in the cute puppy category. He knew all the tricks. 'Attention! Stand up straight!'

As Arlington's ice blue eyes rested on Khan, the proud old dog seemed to stiffen his shoulders, puff his chest out and raise himself a few more centimetres. He stared back at Arlington and held his gaze. The dog next to him lay down. Khan stood firm – the last dog standing.

Khan had done it many times before. All the rosettes he had won over the years were pinned up on a board in Mr Sowerby's study.

Arlington cheered as he placed the rosette on Khan's collar. 'Good old Khan! Still the champion,' he laughed.

That was it. Khan had done his duty and all the other dogs had seen him. He might be old and tired, but he was still a dog to be reckoned with.

 After the agility display, the show was over in the ring. Everyone moved to the other side of the field, to where the drag race was held. The little dogs lined up first. Their owners held them on the start line, while Mikey jiggled the 'rabbit' to get them excited. Ten little tails wagged at top speed as Mikey raised his arm and stuck his thumb up.

They were off! Tumbling over each other, yapping and barking. Mostly they were pugs and miniature poodles. Nando, a chihuahua, surprised everyone. Not only did she win, she disappeared through the hole after the rabbit!

The crowd loved it, cheering, whooping and whistling.

Mikey unwound the rabbit rope for the next category. 'Middle-sized dogs,' he announced.

'That's us!' Walker could feel Stella quivering with excitement as she strained against her leash. They lined up behind some planks of wood that had been laid down to make a start line.

Mikey raised a hand, his thumb went up, the rabbit shot off up the hill, and Stella raced after it. There was no contest. Not only was she fast, she never took her eyes off the rabbit, until it disappeared into the hole and she crashed into the straw bales. The other dogs were yelping way behind her.

Conn, who was standing by the bales, grabbed hold of her and waited for Walker to run up the hill. Stella was beside herself with excitement.

'Did you see me! Did you? Did you?'

'You were amazing!' said Walker.

Stella leaped into his arms and licked his face with her hot, dribbly tongue.

'She's so fast!' said Conn, as he wrote down Stella's name for the prize-giving. 'Ain't nothing gonna stop her, is it? Put her into the all-comers race at the end. I reckon she could win it too! There's some water by the car. Don't let her drink too much or it'll slow her down.'

'Thanks!' said Walker.

Stella lapped the water as if she hadn't drunk any for a week. 'That's enough!' Walker hissed.

They watched the other dogs race, while they waited for the final event. The big dogs lumbered up the hill. Some were a bit ungainly, but they all enjoyed themselves. The working dogs, mostly sheepdogs and terriers, took it all very seriously!

Soon it was time for the all-comers final race. The dogs ranged in size from little Nando to Horatio, an enormous black-and-white spotted Great Dane.

Walker unclipped Stella's lead and held on to her collar. A corgi broke loose, grabbed hold of the rabbit and ran off with it. The crowd were beside themselves with laugher!

In the shade of a tree, bets were secretly being placed on Flash, a silver-grey lurcher who was all legs and hungry, searching eyes. Flash was the dog to beat.

The corgi was rounded up, halfway up the hill, and the rabbit and rope were reset. The crowd hushed as Mikey raised his arm.

 In the back yard of the shop, Boss put his nose to the tiny gap in the fence. He couldn't see what was happening because of the trees in between, but he could smell the excitement.

He could smell all the dogs and hear their barks and cries. They were having such a good time, and here he was stuck in the back yard, guarding, waiting for a bad man to come over the fence. It was never going to happen. He was going to waste his whole life pacing up and down this stupid yard.

He slunk back to his kennel, turned round three times, lay down with his head on his paws and sighed, deeply.

Mikey's arm quivered as he waited for the all-clear signal from the top of the hill.

Walker kept his eye on the rabbit just as keenly as Stella, both waiting for the first twitch of the dummy's ears that would be the sign to start the race. Stella coughed and strained as Walker held her collar to the last second.

The car engine roared into life up the hill, Mikey's thumb went up.

'Steady, girl!' Walker commanded. The other dogs in the line broke their concentration. That was a human talking! A human was speaking dog talk! Their heads turned to see who had spoken, just as the rabbit twitched and began its speedy, jerky journey up the hill.

Walker released his grip and Stella was off like a rocket. 'Go, Stella, go!' he shouted after her.

The other dogs, realising that they had been

left behind, took up the chase, howling and baying. Walker and the other owners followed behind, some walking, some, like Walker, running as fast as they could to get to the top.

'Rabbit! Rabbit!' Stella panted. She never took her eyes of the dummy for a moment. She hurtled up the steepening slope, her heart pounding in her chest, her tongue flailing spit from the corner of her mouth.

The rabbit bumped and jumped over the grass. The sound of the crowd disappeared. All she heard was the singing whine of the rope as it dragged the dummy rabbit up the hill, tantalisingly just too fast for her to catch it.

But she could hear the other dogs coming up behind her. The barking was still distant, but she could sense a rhythm of paws and throaty panting close by. Stella glanced back.

Flash was gaining ground. Flash was huge. Flash looked mean. Flash was so fast! Flash was going to beat her to it!

The wall was getting closer and closer. Stella remembered crashing into the straw wall last time. She skipped a step to shorten her pace, sank low onto her front legs and flung herself into the air.

Her long, fluffy ears streamed behind her, filled with the cheers of the crowd. Her paws grazed the top bale, giving her a little extra height and speed, as she vaulted right over the wall.

She landed just as the dummy rabbit shot through the hole. She heard the thud, thud, thud of the dogs crashing into the bales behind her. Stella threw herself at the rabbit and grabbed it with her teeth. The car engine died, the rabbit stopped and Stella shook it until she was sure that it was dead!

'Stella! Well done!' Walker rounded the bales to see Stella proudly showing off her prey. He sank to his knees, threw his arms around her neck and gave her a huge, hearty hug.

Seconds later they were bombarded by the other dogs, who all wanted to join in the celebration and, more importantly, find out who this boy was that could talk to dogs!

'Well done!' Flash panted. 'I never thought of jumping over the top! That was genius!'

Horatio towered over them all. 'You can speak Dog!' he growled in a deep, gruff voice at Walker.

'Yes,' said Walker. He couldn't think what else to say. He didn't need to say anything, as dogs piled on top of him asking questions, nineteen to the dozen.

Mikey and Conn took in the scene, amazement written all over their faces. Conn puffed his cheeks. 'No doubt who the winner is!'

'I'm not lekking go!' Stella spluttered through the cloth rabbit.

'She's not letting go!' Walker said.

'That's okay,' Mikey laughed, cutting the rabbit off the string with his penknife. 'She's earned it! Stick around for the prize-giving. That's two races she's won!'

Horatio nudged up against Walker. His huge body knocked him off balance, into a ball of excited, admiring terriers who fought each other to lick his face, their tails wagging in an excited line.

The owners peeled their dogs off him one by one, spluttering apologies for their strange behaviour. 'I've never seen anything like it before!' Horatio's owner chuckled. 'You certainly have a way with dogs!'

As Walker struggled to get up, his eyes locked with the familiar icy blue. Arlington Wherewithal was watching him with interest. He'd never seen anything like it before either.

The dog show entry table was now filled with silver cups. A small crowd had gathered around it in a semicircle. Their dogs were hot and tired and mostly slumped on the floor, uninterested in who had won which prize.

Some of the silver cups were a little worse for wear. The winners were allowed to keep them at home for a year, but they had to return them for the next year's competition. Sometimes there would be little accidents while someone was dusting the mantelpiece and the cups would be returned with added dents and scratches.

Walker and Stella, who had not let go of her tartan trophy, stood to one side, watching as the lady with the megaphone announced all the winners.

One by one the owners came up to shake Arlington's hand, receive their cup, be given an envelope and have their photograph taken for the village website news page.

Khan raised a cheer, as he slowly, but proudly, walked forward to receive his prize. He just had to hold out a little longer, show everyone what he was made of, then he could go home and sleep for the rest of the week. He knew his old bones would ache terribly, but it was worth it to keep up his reputation in the village.

Finally, the results of the drag race were announced. The crowd cheered as Nando trotted up to receive his rosette and envelope. There were no cups for the drag race – it wasn't an official part of the dog show, just a bit of fun.

Walker was wondering what the envelopes contained when he heard the jangly, megaphone voice call his and Stella's name.

'I hate that man!' Stella growled through the tartan rabbit.

Walker picked Stella up and went up to the table. He smiled for the crowd and whispered through the side of his mouth. 'Promise me you'll behave yourself?'

Stella grumbled a sort of reply.

Arlington's tight smile suggested menace more than friendliness. 'Ah! It's the dog walker! How's business?'

'Good, thank you, sir.'

Arlington leaned over to place two rosettes on Stella's collar. One for the medium-sized dogs and one for the all-comers race.

'Stella!' he said, in a slimy voice. 'Mrs Little will be so proud of you!'

'Miss,' Walker corrected.

'What? Oh yes.' Arlington picked up two

envelopes, one for each race, and handed them to Walker. 'Smile for the camera, now!'

Walker turned to face the photographer. Several dogs slipped free of their owners and crowded around Walker and Stella. They wanted to be in the picture too. It wasn't every day you met a dog whisperer!

Walker smiled and shrugged his shoulders, as if to say, 'What did I do?' The crowd chuckled and snapped away on their phones.

Walker tried to ignore the dogs, who were chattering away: 'Nice to meet you, Walker – Stella's so lucky – can you take me out for a walk sometime?' A golden retriever sat on his toes and gazed up at him in adoration, as if she had just fallen in love. The crowd sighed with an audible 'Awww!'

'You really do have a way with dogs, don't you?' Arlington said. 'I tell you what, come up to Foxley Manor tomorrow at eleven o'clock. My wife and I are having a few days away in Italy. You can walk my boys for me. How does that sound?'

'Er! Y-yes, sir.' Walker was so surprised he wasn't sure what to say. 'Tomorrow … eleven o'clock,' he sputtered.

'Good! I'll see you then.' Walker was dismissed. Arlington shook hands with the organisers, strode off towards the Manor and was gone.

 'Stella! You clever girl!' Jenny's face lit up when Stella and Walker met her outside the produce tent. 'You won a prize – no! Two.'

Stella dropped the tartan rabbit at Jenny's feet. It was a gift – the spoils of war, won fair and square.

Jenny picked the soggy rabbit up and gave Walker a quizzical look. He explained how Stella had stolen the show in the drag racing event, and how fast she was.

'Well! That's down to all the exercise Walker's been giving you.' Jenny scrunched Stella's face in her hands and kissed the top of her head. 'Did you win a prize?'

Walker took the envelopes out of his back pocket.

'What's inside?' Jenny asked, excitedly.

Walker tore open the envelopes and pulled a card from each.

Jenny made a face. 'Urgh! I wouldn't let Stella eat any of that muck! I just don't trust that man.'

Walker stared at the cards and shrugged. 'I don't think Stella would eat it anyway.'

Jenny had won lots of first-prize cards for her cakes and biscuits and vegetables and flowers. She'd let them all be sold to raise funds for charity and next year's fête, so there wasn't much for her to take home.

Walking back to Jenny's house, Walker felt really guilty when he told her that he'd agreed to walk Arlington's dogs. It was like playing for another team.

'Well.' Jenny took a deep breath. 'That's between you and him. Personally I wouldn't trust that man as far as I could throw him. Make sure you charge him lots of money!'

'But he does so much to help dogs,' Walker said. 'He can't be all bad, can he?' Walker had read a display at the dog show that explained how Arlington's dog food business sponsored dog rescue sanctuaries all around the country. And how Arlington had been showered with awards for his work with dogs. His pointers were champions! There was even an old picture of him with Queen Elizabeth and her corgis!

Tired and full of cake, he gave Stella a big hug goodbye and went home.

But first he needed to stop by the shop. Boss sensed him coming and was waiting by the gate. A look passed between them. Walker smiled as he opened the door.

'I saw this and thought of you,' he said, giving Anje a blue, striped paper bag.

She looked at the bag, then at Walker, then at her dad. 'Come along!' her dad laughed. 'Let's see!'

Anje opened the bag and pulled out a cellophane envelope that contained a badge. It was yellow and black. Around the top it said, 'Watch out, there's an...' then there was an embroidered silhouette of an Alsatian dog and the word 'about!' below.

'It looks just like Boss!' Anje gasped. She couldn't think what else to say. Walker felt suddenly embarrassed. His mouth went dry and he couldn't think of anything to say either.

Mr Bonus broke the silence. 'Is true!' he chuckled. 'Look just like Boss! You can put it on your jacket with other badges. Say thank you, Anje!'

Anje nodded and managed a whisper. 'Thanks!'

Walker turned to Mr Bonus. 'Actually, I wanted to ask your advice.' He explained about Arlington and how he had been summoned to the Foxley Manor.

Anje's eyes opened wide. 'Are you going there on your own?'

'I suppose so,' Walker replied. 'It's business, after all.' Then he asked, 'But how much should I charge?'

'Simple,' Mr Bonus stood up straight, in his business-like pose. 'You want to do this walking job for Mister Arlington?'

'Not really. He just sort of told me I had to do it, without asking me first.'

'Okay,' Mr Bonus nodded. 'This is what you do. Think how much you do job for, then double the price. He no like the price, you no do the job. He like the price, at least you get paid good!'

A little light went on in Walker's brain and he smiled. It was so simple when Mr Bonus explained it.

'Ha!' Mr Bonus patted him on the back. 'You make good businessman!'

'Who's the Boss?' Walker whispered, quietly, as he stepped lightly past the gate at the side of the shop.

On the other side of the gate Boss growled, 'Me! I'm the

Boss!' Walker laughed, leaving Boss wagging his tail, feeling happier than he had for a long time.

 The words, Foxley Manor, were carved into the stone gateway to Arlington's estate. A small, hand-painted sign beneath announced that it was PRIVATE.

Walker felt that the whole village must be watching, as he walked up the long, winding drive.

The imposing stone building rose up in front of him. Roses rambled across the facade. The porch was a mess of walking boots and umbrellas. Walker couldn't see a bell anywhere. A brass lion's head glared at him. It held a heavy brass ring in its mouth. Walker reached up and knocked three times.

He heard a voice inside call over the yapping of a tiny dog, 'It's okay, darling. I've got it!' The heavy door opened on squeaking hinges. Arlington stared down at Walker.

'Ah! It's you. Come along!' Arlington closed the

door briskly behind him and strode off, leading Walker round to a courtyard at the back of the house. 'The kennels are round here.'

The kennels were at the end of a stable block, built in the same style as the main house. Walker heard horses whinnying somewhere inside. Arlington took a key from his pocket and gave it to him.

'Here, you'd better have this. Don't lose it. Now, let's see what they make of you!'

Arlington stood to one side, and leaned casually against the wall.

Walker realised it was a test. He spoke soothingly to the dogs, as he slipped the key into the lock, opened the gate and entered the kennel yard.

Arlington's pair of pointers immediately wagged their tails and bounced around him, licking his hands and snuffing their greetings.

'Good Lord!' Arlington exclaimed. 'You really do have a way with dogs, don't you? Sit!' he ordered in a firm voice.

The dogs obeyed at once. They bowed their heads, ashamed. For a moment they'd forgotten they were gun dogs, not pets!

'These are Thor and Loki,' Arlington said.

'Cool!' said Walker. 'Like the Marvel heroes?'

'What?' Arlington looked confused. 'They're named after the Viking gods! I have Viking heritage, you know?'

Walker remembered doing something about Vikings at school.

'You'll need to come and walk them once a day for at least an hour. Don't go off the estate, I don't want them mixing with village dogs. They know their way around. Stick to the path and you can't get lost. If they get wet or dirty, you can rub them down with a towel in the tack room.' He led Walker into the building next door.

The tack room smelled of leather and sweet hay. It was full of horsey things – saddles, bridles, brushes and blankets. Horses were a world he knew little about. He could see inside the stable and hear them shifting in their boxes.

'Here are their leads, said Arlington. 'I never take them, but you'd better carry them just in case.' Arlington puffed his cheeks out. 'Okay. To business. How much? We'll be away for four days.'

Walker had calculated and recalculated how much to charge, then he'd doubled it, but that sounded too much, so he halved it again. 'Ten pounds!' he blurted out.

'Ha!' Arlington laughed. 'You've got a nerve! Ten pounds a day? That's daylight robbery. I'll pay you five pounds a day. Start tomorrow and we'll be home on Thursday evening.'

Walker was shocked. There was no spitting and shaking hands with Arlington, you just did as you were told. *Did he say five pounds a day?*

Arlington escorted Walker back to the drive. 'Mrs Scowles, my housekeeper, will be looking after the place and feeding the boys. I'll let Mr Scowles know you are coming. Osmo is my gamekeeper. He looks after the estate, so don't go upsetting him.'

As Walker turned to go, he hesitated. 'Today is the last day of the holidays,' Walker explained. 'After today, I can only come after school, so is it okay to bring Stella with me? I walk her every day.'

Arlington screwed up his eyes and studied the boy closely. Was this a deal breaker?

'Oh. All right,' he nodded, 'but make sure she behaves herself.'

'We knew you could talk to us!' Loki said, excitedly.

It was Monday afternoon, and Walker was introducing the dogs to each other at Foxley Manor. 'Stella … this is Thor and Loki.'

'Well, hello!' said Thor, sniffing Stella's neck.

'Stop it! That tickles!' Stella giggled.

Walker took the leads off a hook on the wall.

'We don't need those,' Thor laughed. 'We'll look after you. Come on!'

The pointers bounced across the courtyard.

They stood proud and tall by the side gate, full of restrained energy, waiting to get going.

Stella watched them. 'I promise I'll behave too,' she said.

'Okay,' Walked laughed. He unclipped her lead and opened the gate. 'Let's go.'

The three dogs raced across the enormous lawn in front of the house, leaping on top of each other, chasing each other's tails, barking for joy!

'No-o-o-o!' Walker shouted. It was too late. All three dogs ran straight for the lake and plunged in, barking and splashing. Sunlight glittered on the water.

'No-o-o-o!' Walker shouted again! Again it was too late. All three dogs ran straight up to him, stopped, tensed their shoulders and shook a cascade of water into the air, soaking him and creating miniature rainbows that danced in front of him.

'Wait till I get you!' Walker ran after the trio, who bounced off towards the woods, barking with laughter and joy.

'Don't go too far ahead!' Walker called. The dogs bounded back, running around him in circles, jumping up and licking his face.

'Come on, slowcoach!' Loki laughed. Then they were off again.

Stella tipped her head. 'Boys!' she giggled. 'What do you expect?' Then, with a gleeful bark, she ran off to join them in a new game.

Thor and Loki led the way around the estate, running ahead and returning to urge Walker not be such a slowcoach. They went past the rocky spot where they and Arlington had first met.

'We knew you were different, even then,' said Thor.

'Yes, there was something about the way you

were with Stella,' Loki agreed, before they bounced off again in search of smells and small creatures to chase.

Walker followed the path, all the way through the woods on the estate, right around the top of the house and back again.

He could see the house up ahead and waited for the dogs to catch him up. It was so peaceful. He let the sun warm his back, drying the last of the dampness from the soaking he'd had by the lake. Birds whistled and twittered. He could just hear the rumble of traffic in the distance. And … what was that other noise?

A warm, gentle breeze blew through the woods, carrying with it the faintest sound. A soft, gentle sound, like a dandelion seed floating effortlessly on the air.

So faint. So weak. So plaintive! He couldn't think what it was, but he understood the message in it. No, not a message … a feeling … an emotion…

A plea for help!

Then he heard something else. Hairs prickled on the back of his neck. Walker spun round.

'What're you doing nosin' round here?' Osmo Scowles, the gamekeeper, stood there, glaring, holding a shot gun. His Jack Russell, Bolt, growled. Osmo pointed his gun right at Walker's chest.

 Not far away, a tiny baby pug crawled towards its mother. It wasn't well. The mother licked it all over, trying to force health back into the mewling pup. It was weak, not like its brothers and sisters, who were struggling

and clambering over each other to get the best position for more milk. This pup hadn't fed for hours. A runny mess of sticky tears ringed its enormous, baleful eyes.

Once, the mother had had a name, but that was long ago, from a time she could barely remember. She sighed. Another nameless mother, in a crate across the room, watched her through the bars with sad, defeated eyes.

'I-I'm not nosing around.' Walker stumbled over his words. His eyes were glued to the shotgun. A shaky, quivery feeling gripped and twisted his insides.

Loki, Thor and Stella ran back along the path behind Walker. Taking in the situation, they raced to his aid, mustering in front of their friend, protecting him from Osmo.

'Don't trust him,' Loki told Walker. 'Or Bolt, he's only interested in rats and fighting.'

Bolt growled. Osmo narrowed his eyes and dropped the gun to his side. 'Oh, yeah. Now I remember. Mister Wherewithal said you'd be coming by to walk the dogs. You make sure you stick to the path, and don't go nosin' round this side of the estate.'

'Yes, sir! I-I mean no, sir. I shan't.' Walker backed away towards the courtyard and the kennels. 'Come on, let's get you boys cleaned up,' he called, but the dogs held their ground, watching Osmo melt away into the trees.

On the fading breeze again were those faint, eerie, mournful cries.

Loki turned his head towards the sound. 'Can you hear it?' he asked.

'Yes,' said Walker. 'What is it?'

'I don't know,' said Thor, 'but I'd like to find out. Those sounds haunt us when the winds blows in this direction.'

Loki looked thoughtful as Walker brushed the mud off their sleek coats. 'Can you smell it?'

Walker stopped brushing. 'What?'

'Chemicals,' Loki sniffed. 'It smells of bleach and cleaning fluids. But it doesn't quite mask the scent of fear.'

Behind the church, at the end of the path that connected the village green to Foxley Fields, the man who had been surveying Jenny Little's garden with Arlington Wherewithal all those weeks before hammered a stake into the ground and stapled a notice to it.

Underneath was a map of Foxley Fields with plans for twenty-three houses and three paragraphs of tiny writing that explained that if anyone was not happy about the situation, they should lodge a complaint at the council offices.

The man, Crispin Lightfoot, moved on. Silently, he opened the gate to Number 34 the High Street. He'd waited till Walker was walking the dogs, so that Stella wasn't there to bark a warning. The man stepped lightly to the front door and pushed a thick envelope through the letterbox.

Jenny heard it drop onto the mat, but by the time she reached the door and picked up the letter, the man had gone.

Time for him to put the notices up around the village and plan the next phase of the operation.

When he brought Stella back, Jenny was in tears. Stella ran to her and nuzzled her hands.

'What's the matter?' Walker felt awkward. It was unsettling to see grown-ups cry.

She held a letter in her hand. 'That man!' she wailed, tossing the letter on the kitchen table.

Walker couldn't help seeing the heading that was printed in bold, red letters.

Notice of Eviction

He felt useless. 'Is there anything I can do?' he asked.

She smiled and dropped her shoulders, a gesture of helplessness. 'I don't think you can,' she said. 'Not unless you know how to get rid of Arlington Wherewithal! He claims that my house is built on his property and I have to be out by the end of the month!'

'But...' Walker didn't understand. It didn't make sense.

'And then,' Jenny continued, 'he's going to knock it down so he can build a load of houses all over Foxley Fields!'

'He can't do that!' Walker looked at the clock. 'I'd better get home,' he said. 'I'll tell my mum, she's on the council, she might be able to help.'

'It looks like the council have agreed to it already.' Tears welled up in Jenny's eyes again. 'The council will do anything that Arlington tells them.'

Walker sidled towards the door. 'I'll see you tomorrow,' he said. 'Look after her, Stella.'

Stella nodded.

His mum had sent him a message to pick up some ketchup from the shop on his way home. Walker got a bottle of ketchup off the shelf and took it to the counter to pay.

'Hey, Walker! This bad business for you, eh?' Mr Bonus pointed to a poster that had been sellotaped to the door.

'Look, here's a leaflet about it.'

Walker paid for the ketchup and read the leaflet as he ambled along the pavement. Boss huffed a greeting as he walked past the side gate. Walker looked up. Anje was standing in the yard.

'Hi, there,' she said. 'Have you done your homework?'

She saw the leaflet in Walker's hand. 'Oh! Everyone has been going on about that in the shop today. That Mister Arlington Wherewithal has really got everyone fired up.'

'That Mister Arlington Wherewithal is a bad man!' Walker mumbled.

Boss narrowed his eyes. The sound of the words, '*bad man*,' made him growl.

'See ya.' Walker needed to get home.

'See ya!' Anje peered through the gate, watching Walker cross the road and disappear around the corner.

'We need to go to this!' Walker said, slamming the leaflet on the kitchen table. 'It's important!'

As Mum read, her eyebrows tightened into a frown.

Walker felt helpless. Words came tumbling out of his mouth. 'Arlington Wherewithal wants to knock down Jenny's house and build a huge load of houses. That can't be right, can it? He can't do that!'

He had to try to do something. Going to the meeting was a start.

'He'll build on Foxley Fields over my dead body!' Mum snarled, when she finished reading. As they ate supper, Walker told her about the letter Jenny had received – how Arlington was going to pull her house down.

'He can't!' said Mum. 'There's a preservation order on her house. It's of historical importance!'

'That reminds me,' said Dad, 'There's a programme of historical importance I wanted to watch on TV. It's about World War One,' he explained, as he picked up Lucy Lou and sidled out of the kitchen.

'Wait for the meeting,' his mum told him. 'Nothing is final yet.'

For the next three days, Walker took the dogs out after school. With the giant lawn to play on, he took his ball launcher too. They loved it, racing across the grass to try to catch the ball before it bounced. Even though the pointers had longer legs, Stella was so fast she often beat them to it.

Thor and Loki loved it best when Walker threw the ball high into the air over the lake. A small, wooden fishing jetty jutted out into the reeds. Leaping off the end of it, they launched themselves skyward, crashing into the water, creating fountains of spray and turbulent waves, as the ball plummeted into the lake.

Of course Stella joined in the fun too. Each day, the dogs would end up covered in leaves, their fur caked in stinking, slimy mud from the lake. Walker had to hose them down in the courtyard and rub them dry with towels.

Stella returned home a little damp each day. Jenny didn't mind. She liked to see Stella happy with new friends, even if the pointers did belong to Arlington Wherewithal. Anyway, her mind was on other things.

On Thursday afternoon, as Walker and Stella were arriving up the drive, Osmo passed them in his old, battered Land Rover. Bolt sat up, with his paws on the dashboard, staring out of the windscreen. Osmo's cruel eyes narrowed, studying Walker, as he stood to one side, letting the vehicle pass.

The vaguest hint of autumn tinged the air,

sweet, apply aromas from the fallen fruit in the orchard. Damp, fungal smells filtered through the woods and strong gusts of wind blew the first, yellowing leaves from the trees.

As they neared the end of their walk, a fierce blast of wind rustled through the trees, carrying with it the distinct howl of a dog in pain. Not physical pain, but the pain of loss and desperation.

A look passed between the dogs. The pointers faced into the wind, smelling both the chemical reek and the animal scent of fear and something even more dreadful. They turned to Walker.

'Someone needs help!' growled Thor. 'Let's go!'

 Close by, the mother pug, the one with no name, nudged her sixth puppy with her nose, trying to warm its lifeless body, urging it to wake up. It was no use. It was her desperate cry of pain and bewilderment that Walker and the dogs had heard. And the cry of all the other mothers in their crates, howling for the litters they had borne and lost over the years.

 Crashing through the undergrowth, Walker ignored the signs tacked onto the trees: *Private! Trespassers will be prosecuted!* It was okay, Osmo wasn't about.

A clearing opened up in the woods. A thin wisp of smoke drifted from the chimney of a small cottage. The sign on the gate read: Keeper's Cottage.

This must be where Osmo and Mrs Scowles live, Walker thought.

At the bottom of the vegetable garden, a ramshackle arrangement of sheds hung together like rotting teeth. They were surrounded by a high fence that crackled with electricity.

This was the source of the heart-rending cries. Now Walker could smell what the dogs had too – that smell of the boys' toilets after school, when the cleaners had just been in and the floors were still wet with bleach. And something else – a dirty, unwashed, uncared-for smell, mixed with stale dog wee and poo.

'Here! Round the back!' Loki called.

Walker skirted round the yard, keeping clear of the house, in case Mrs Scowles was at home and watching.

'What is it?' he whispered, as he caught up with Loki, Thor and Stella.

The sheds had been added, one to another, over the years, to make one long shed with different sized rooms and connecting doors. The windows were barred, the doors double-padlocked. The windows at the back were all boarded up. All except one. Thor pointed his nose towards this tiny window. It was more an air vent really.

It was a bit too high for Walker to see in. He looked around for something to stand on. The area behind the shed was a dumping-ground. Among the garden waste, he found an old plastic bucket and turned it upside down against the wall.

Walker stood on it, pulled himself up and peered in. A stench of warm, stale air poured out of the vent onto Walker's face. It wasn't air, it felt more like a thick, clammy, dirty liquid. Walker blinked his eyes.

He knew exactly what he was looking at. He'd seen videos and news reports on the TV, but that didn't help to overcome the shock of seeing the real thing.

The dingy light revealed wooden crates, old packing cases with cage wire strapped across their open fronts. Each contained a little family of dogs. On the floor, in the larger crates, were the bigger dogs: retrievers, golden labradors and poodles. Above them, stacked up to the ceiling, were all the popular smaller breeds, spaniels, terriers, Westies, a boxer, a dachshund, a Pomeranian and, almost out of sight, a pug, howling at a tiny, lifeless shape that lay on the stained sleeping bag that was the little family's bed.

Rage welled up inside Walker, like molten lava boiling inside a volcano. His eyes blurred, filling with tears of anger and frustration. What could he do? He had to tell someone about this. He had to expose this awful place and the people responsible for it.

But no one would ever believe him. Arlington Wherewithal was a pillar of the community. He was famous for looking after dogs. No one would ever believe he had a puppy farm on his land.

They'd believe it if he had evidence!

Walker pulled his phone from his pocket and began filming. He was concentrating so hard, he didn't hear the sound of Osmo crashing the gears and revving the engine of the old Land Rover, as he swerved off the road and drove through the gates at the bottom of the drive.

The dogs were jumping up at him, but Walker just thought they wanted to know what he was filming through the vent.

Osmo turned off the drive and clattered down the pot-holed track that led to Keeper's Cottage.

'It's Osmo!' Loki hissed. 'Quick! Let's get out of here!'

The Land Rover slid to a dusty halt.

'Come on!' Stella urged.

The car door slammed shut and Osmo's feet crunched across the gravel.

Finally Walker heard him. He froze.

Bolt barked. The footsteps stopped. The wind dropped.

Walker had never experienced such silence. His heart thumped in his chest, like a sledgehammer pounding inside him. It was so loud he thought Osmo would surely hear it. His throat tightened with fear, his breath became shallow.

'Who's there?' Had Osmo seen them?

'Come on, Walker! Let's get out of here!' Stella rocked from leg to leg, tense, frightened. 'Now, before it's too late!'

Gently, Walker turned to ease himself down from the bucket. His sweatshirt was caught on a rusty nail. Drat! He raised himself a little, to unhook it. The bucket was old and the plastic was brittle. As he stood on tiptoe, all his weight was concentrated in one weak spot.

'CRACK!' The bucket shattered into pieces. It was as if someone had pulled a rug from underneath him. Walker threw a hand out to break his fall. *Don't let go of the phone,* he

thought, as he landed in a patch of stinging
nettles. The phone was his evidence.

'Run!' Stella was by his side, pushing him with
her nose.

'Come out right now!' Osmo's angry voice
called. 'I know you're there and I know who you
are! I'm calling the police!'

Stella was desperate! 'NOW!' she growled.

Walker jumped up and threw himself into a low, ground-hugging run and chased after her.

Stella followed the scent that Thor and Loki had laid through the woods. Osmo's angry shouts rang out behind them. Walker's entire being concentrated on running away from danger. Twice he tripped and stumbled over a root or a twisty, trailing bramble. Each time he rolled and picked himself up in one swift, flowing move, sprinting onwards, through the newly fallen leaves and prickly chestnut skins. His panicked gasps seemed to ring out across the woodland floor. Keep running! Keep running! Don't stop!

'Here!' called Thor. 'Hide round here. Get your breath back and we can join the path above the house and make it look as if we're coming from the other direction.'

Walker thought his chest would explode. Would he ever be able to breathe normally again? Would he ever stop feeling so scared?

Slowly his body calmed. He wiped his fingers on his sweatshirt and stuck them in his mouth.

The nettle stings throbbed. Small white lumps had swelled on the red, angry skin. He touched the sore spot above his eye and saw blood on his fingers! He'd cut himself. His sweatshirt had a rip in it from the nail. He must look a mess!

Walker gathered his thoughts and tried to clean himself up. He smoothed down his sweatshirt and brushed the leaves and green stains from his jeans. Something didn't feel right. His pocket was empty.

'My phone!' he gasped. 'No one will believe me if I don't have the pictures!'

'Good Lord! What happened to you?' Arlington's car purred to a halt, just as Walker and the dogs arrived back in the courtyard. Thor and Loki bounced up to their master, snuffing and squealing their greetings.

Walker felt shaky seeing Arlington after all he'd found out today. He looked down at his clothes. 'Oh! The dogs went in the lake. S-sorry, I'll go and clean them up.'

When he came out of the tack room, having cleaned up all three dogs, he saw Arlington deep in conversation with Osmo and another man. The man was showing a folder of papers to Arlington. Something made them laugh in a hearty, haughty way. Osmo stood to one side, keeping a respectful distance, casting sideways glances at Walker. Bolt growled at him.

Walker felt his cheeks burning. Osmo must know it was him at the puppy farm. He quietly locked Thor and Loki into the kennel and said goodbye. It wasn't likely that Arlington would ask him to look after them again, was it?

Arlington pulled a twenty pound note from his wallet. 'Here you are!' He held it out like bait in a trap. He held it a little too tightly. Walker had to tug it to release it from his grasp.

'Well, the dogs look healthy,' Arlington smiled. 'Thanks for all your hard work.'

He held Walker with his piercing blue eyes, searching for something. Walker felt his cheeks flush. He dropped his gaze.

'Thank you,' he whispered, tucking the note into his pocket ... his empty pocket! What was he going to do about his phone? His throat was dry. 'C-c-come along, Stella. Let's get you home.'

The men's cold laughter followed him down the drive.

That evening, on the way to the meeting at the village hall, Walker went to pick up Jenny and Stella, as they had arranged. Mum wanted to go too, but she knew the hall would be full of Foxley Field dog walkers and their dogs.

'Apparently my house is not historically important enough,' said Jenny.

Her eyes were red from crying. 'I can't face coming to the meeting tonight,' she said. 'Everyone will be watching me and asking questions. I'm not ready for that.'

'Well, I'm still going,' said Walker. 'Can I take Stella with me? We should show our support.' Stella had already picked up her lead and was waiting by the front door. 'I'll bring her back on my way home, afterwards.'

As he headed to the meeting, he noticed that lots of people were arriving with their dogs. Walker had an idea. 'Stella,' he said, 'I'm going to need your help.'

The village hall was full of angry people talking nineteen to the dozen. No one wanted to see houses built on Foxley Fields and they wanted to make sure everyone else understood the strength of their feelings.

Geoff and Pam Sowerby sat behind a table at the front. Khan lay down on the floor beside them. However old he was, he had to show that he was still up for the fight. Khan had spent many happy times running around Foxley Fields when he was younger and fitter. He wouldn't want that experience to be denied to new generations of Foxley village dogs.

Geoff rang a little bell. The gentle tinkle had an instant calming effect. The crowd of people bustled into their seats as Geoff took control of the meeting.

The villagers were angry. One by one they let off steam, waving placards and calling Arlington Wherewithal all sorts of names. One by one they told how much Foxley Fields meant to them, but no one seemed to have any ideas, no one knew what to do. Arlington was rich and important – he had powerful friends in high places.

'Psst!' Stella was trying to attract Khan's attention. 'Psst!'

The old dog raised an eyebrow. 'Psst!' Stella waggled her eyebrows and nodded towards the back of the hall. The old dog frowned. Stella waggled her ears and waved her nose. Finally,

Khan seemed to understand. He heaved himself to his feet and quietly padded down the aisle.

Geoff and Pam were used to Khan wandering off. He wouldn't go far. He couldn't … he was too old and much too tired.

'Come on,' Stella whispered. 'We need you.'

Walker eased the doors open and let the two dogs into a small lobby at the back of the hall.

'What's this all about?' Khan asked.

'We have to take matters into our own paws,' said Stella. 'Those humans are never going to decide anything, and we have an even more important problem to sort out.'

She told Khan what they had discovered that afternoon. Walker explained what he had seen through the little window at the puppy farm and how he was sure that Arlington knew that he knew the terrible secret.

'But I lost my phone with the evidence on it.' Walker sighed. 'Somehow we have to get the police involved.'

The more he heard, the more Khan seemed to come alive. Their story fired his sense of injustice. You could almost see his mind at work, plotting, planning, working out what actions they might take.

Finally he nodded. 'Remember the end of *One Hundred and One Dalmatians*?' he asked.

'You know that movie?' Walker was surprised.

Stella rolled her eyes. 'We all love that movie. I know it off by heart!' She turned to Khan. 'Do you mean the twilight call? When all the dogs start barking, sending a message across London?'

'That's it.' Khan nodded. 'We need to do something like that. We need the help of every dog in the village. Many of them are here tonight.

We need them all to break free tomorrow at six and meet up at Foxley Fields. I'll give everyone instructions there.'

The doors opened. The meeting was over and people began to leave.

'We need your help,' Stella and Khan told the other dogs as they walked past with their owners. 'Break free and meet up in Foxley Fields at six o'clock tomorrow evening. This is very important – be there and tell any other dog you meet.'

The dog owners of Foxley were perplexed that night. Their dogs seemed excited. Maybe it was the full moon having a weird effect on them?

A very nervous Jenny Little opened the door to Walker and Stella. 'How did the meeting go?'

'Oh, okay,' Walker nodded. 'We have a sort of plan. I need to take Stella out again at six o'clock tomorrow evening. Is that okay?'

Stella wagged her tail and gave her the look that Jenny found impossible to say no to. 'Yes, okay. I'll see you tomorrow, then. Night, night.'

Khan was old and tired, but this new project had fired him up. The village needed him. It would take a while to get to Foxley Fields. He needed to be the first to arrive, in case some of the younger, more excitable dogs went off without proper instructions.

At a quarter past five, Khan picked up his lead, just as he used to when he was younger. He padded down the hallway, sat down on the welcome mat by the front door and began to howl.

Pam and Geoff looked up from their ipads and stared at each other. 'What's the matter with Khan? said Geoff.

Pam leaned back in her stress-free recliner chair, stretching her neck to see round the door frame. Her jaw dropped in astonishment. 'I don't believe it. He wants to go for a walk!'

'What?' Geoff was thrilled to see Khan so animated. He was even making an effort to wag his tail! 'Come on then, boy,' Geoff said. 'Let's go and get some fresh air.'

Khan led the way down the garden path. Phase one of the plan was underway!

Khan seemed to know where he was going, so Geoff let him take the lead. He was old. He had earned the choice.

Similar scenes were unfolding all around the village. Dogs who had received the message were howling by front doors, begging to be taken for a walk. The moment they saw their chance – the moment their owners lost concentration, the moment the grip on their leads loosened for a second, they were off!

All over the village, dogs were leaping over walls, scrabbling under fences and crashing through hedges. They came from all directions, all of them heading for Foxley Fields.

At ten to six, as Walker left Jenny's house with Stella, a river of dogs ran past her front gate. 'Hey, Stella, this is the best fun ever!' Pixie yapped, as she ran along the pavement, tripping up the feet of bigger dogs.

'What is going on?!' Jenny looked alarmed.

'It's okay,' Walker reassured her. 'We need to get to Foxley Fields by six. I'll tell you all about it later.'

Jenny shook her head as she watched them go. She couldn't say no. An incredible bond had grown between Stella and this boy, who seemed to have made such an impact on their lives in such a short time.

 On the corner of Hazel Drive, Benjie was desperate. His owner was always late home, but this was ridiculous! Benjie was going to miss all the action. In his frustration, he had destroyed four letters, a double-glazing advert, three magazines, a tea towel and a pot plant, that he'd knocked over by mistake. The hallway was knee-deep in leaves, potting compost and shredded paper.

At five minutes to six, he heard the front gate click. Hooray! His owner was home. The key slid into the lock. As soon as the door was open wide enough, Benjie squeezed through and was off like greased lightning, down Hazel Drive, across the High Street, making a learner driver do an emergency stop before they'd ever been taught how to.

Boss was pacing up and down by the shop side gate. He heard Benjie's claws skittering along the pavement and called out to know what was happening. Boss felt so left out, locked up in his concrete yard. Something big was going on and he wasn't part of it.

'Can't stop!' Benjie yapped, as he skidded round the corner, taking the short cut through the church yard, weaving in and out of the gravestones to the tumbled-down section of wall that brought him out into Foxley Fields.

'I'm not late, am I?' he barked.

 Geoff Sowerby had no idea what was going on. Khan was surrounded by twenty or thirty dogs of every kind and size. It was like the starting line of the all-comers drag race at the village fête. They listened intently, as Khan ruffed, barked and growled his instructions.

'That man, Arlington Wherewithal, is running a horrible puppy farm on the Foxley Manor Estate.'

Khan began. 'We are going to save those poor imprisoned mothers and their puppies.'

The audience broke into a cacophony of tales about Arlington. None of the dogs liked him.

Pixie shivered. 'The way he pulls you about when he's judging – it makes me want to bite him! But he's so scary, I wouldn't dare.'

'And his eyes are so cruel!' said Benjie.

'And Arlington's Chumpkin Chunks taste disgusting!' said Tucker, an overweight mix of

collie and Dobermann. 'But that's all my owners ever feed me.'

Khan held up his paw and calmed the crowd. 'Here's what we are going to do,' he said. 'Listen carefully. This could be dangerous, so stick to the plan.'

'What *is* going on?' Geoff called across to Walker, who was crouched next to Stella. He knew the dogs would listen to Khan more than him.

'Don't worry, Mister Sowerby,' he said, reassuringly. 'Khan has everything under control!'

By now, anxious owners were pouring into Foxley Fields, waving leads and calling their dogs.

'Quick, Khan,' Stella called. 'We need to get going!'

'Does everyone understand what to do?' Khan asked.

'WOOOF!' The dogs roared their reply.

'Then go – and everyone stick to the plan!'

The band of village dogs raced towards Foxley Manor. Their owners, who had only just caught up with them, collapsed, breathless and confused. What was going on? Their dogs seemed to be under some mysterious spell. It was like a kind of mass hypnosis! Now that their pets were disappearing into the trees, they'd never catch them.

'Someone – call – the – police!' Ellie Snapchat panted, as she collapsed onto the dewy grass.

 Walker and Stella ran up the hill and made their way to the top of the estate so they could come round behind the kennels without being seen.

All around them dogs were barking. The plan was for them to scatter across the estate, then bark and run, bark and run, to cause confusion and make it sound like the woods were filled with hundreds of wild dogs. Stella ran ahead to tell Thor and Loki what was happening.

'Hide!' said Thor. 'Arlington's coming.'

Arlington was in a terrible mood. 'What the hell is going on?' he roared into the fading light. 'Come on, you two!' he snarled, as he opened the kennel door. 'Come with me. I'm not having anyone trespassing on my land!'

'I managed to tell Thor and Loki what's happening,' said Stella, when Walker caught up with her. 'But Arlington has taken them with him.'

In the distance, Arlington swore and shouted something, then two loud blasts echoed through the trees.

'Flippin' heck!' Walker swore.

Far, far in the distance, Stella heard police sirens, 'They're coming,' she said. As they came closer, Walker soon heard them too.

'Come on,' he whispered. 'We'll take the long way round to the rendezvous point.'

Soon the woods were alive with the intense flash of blue lights. Crazy, momentary shadows flickered across the tree trunks, making confusing, abstract patterns on the leaves. Sirens wailed. Dog owners called their pet's names. Everywhere, dogs were barking. The police sirens were the signal they'd been waiting for. Khan had told them Walker's plan: that they make for the puppy farm at Keeper's Cottage and to bark, bark, bark, drawing the police in that direction.

The breeze was blowing towards them. That unmistakable smell of fear filled Stella's nostrils, making her more determined than ever to see the end of Arlington Wherewithal's evil handiwork.

The salty smell of gunpowder stung Walker's nose.

Walker and Stella peered around the side of the shed. Osmo and Arlington were arguing, silhouetted by the porch light at the side of Keeper's Cottage. Thor and Loki paced up and down beside them, agitated, raising their heads to the fast-dimming sky, joining in the chorus of barks and howls.

'Yes!' Walker hissed. 'They're joining in.'

Torches flashed. Bold voices shouted orders. 'This is the police – everyone stop where you are!'

Osmo and Arlington ignored the command. They took off into the shadows, hoping to slip away through the hidden paths at the back of the estate.

Osmo collided with Loki, tripped and fell. 'Boom!' His shotgun went off as it landed on the path. Walker felt a rush of wind above his head. The shot from the blast scattered into the trees above him. Scraps of leaves and twigs fluttered down to the ground.

Walker's heart missed several beats. This was really dangerous!

'You're nicked!' the police shouted, as they jumped on top of Osmo, slamming handcuffs on his wrist.

Arlington crashed through the undergrowth, where Walker and Stella were taking cover. Arlington froze as he came face to face with them. 'YOU!' he growled. 'This is all your fault, you meddling little...' The shotgun trembled in his hands as anger overwhelmed him.

A shape lunged out of the darkness. Thor hit Arlington hard, grabbing his arm firmly in his teeth.

'Get down!' Arlington ordered.

Loki grabbed a leg. Arlington had never been a kind master. Thor and Loki ignored the orders they would once have obeyed without question.

Arlington swung the butt of the gun at Loki, hitting him hard on the head. Loki yelped with the pain. Shocked, Thor let go his grip. It was enough. Dropping his gun, Arlington sprang away, into the gathering darkness.

'Loki! Are you alright?' Walker held the dog's head in his lap. A deep gash on Loki's head was weeping dark, sticky blood. Walker pulled his sleeve up over his hand and pressed it firmly on the wound.

'You get help for Loki,' said Stella. 'We're faster.'

'Yes,' Walker had to agree. He looked into Stella's eyes, overcome by how serious this had all become. 'Don't let him get away.'

Stella obeyed. 'Come on, Thor.' Both dogs ran into the dark.

No one knew his master's scent like Thor did. Arlington was scared and leaving a particularly easy trail to follow.

'Quick, he's trying to get to the car. We've got to head him off!'

Stella and Thor raced ahead of him, taking up their position between Arlington and the big, sleek SUV parked in the courtyard.

Arlington's face was scratched and bleeding, leaves and twigs were caught up in his long, wild hair.

Stella and Thor growled and bared their teeth. There was no way they were letting him get near the car.

Arlington saw the hatred on the dogs' faces and made a quick decision. Changing direction, he was off again, through the side gate and across the lawn towards the lake and the path that followed along behind the houses on the High Street.

If he could just get away from the police. He was rich. He had friends in high places. If he could just get away, he'd be able to sort this all out!

'Khan! Where are you?' Geoff Sowerby was alarmed by the shouts and sirens and gunfire. He'd gone to the edge of the field to peer into the woods to see what was happening. When he turned round, Khan had gone! 'How!?' Khan was so slow, he couldn't have gone far, but which direction?

Khan was running – actually running! He would pay for it tomorrow. His old bones would ache like nothing he had known before, but there was a job to be done and he wasn't going to fail in his duty. He had to get down to the path behind the High Street to make sure that particular escape route had been covered.

And here he was! That man who had manhandled and belittled him at all the dog shows over the years. That man who could look at you as if he was choosing which joint of meat to have for Sunday lunch. That man, Arlington, was running towards him on the path.

Khan stood his ground. He bared his teeth and, with all the rage and hatred he had for a man who could cause such distress to mothers and puppies, he snarled, letting his teeth flash in the cold light of the full moon that was just now rising over Foxley Fields.

'Khan!' Arlington froze. Fear blazed all over his face. Thor and Stella skidded to a halt behind him, snarling their hatred too.

The fence. Get over the fence. It was the one thought left in Arlington's head. The fence was only chest high. Arlington began to raise himself up.

'GRRRRRR.' Google did not like this man. Google ran up the garden path and crashed into the French windows, barking to let her owners know that they were being invaded. Then he turned and raced back down to the bottom of the garden, hurling himself at the fence!

Arlington was so surprised, he lost his balance and fell back into the brambles.

Google was so surprised at his bravery, he ran and hid under the barbecue cover.

Arlington picked himself up, ripping his jacket on the thorns. He backed away from the dogs. Another fence. Next door. He could climb it. He would be safe on the other side.

There was rusty barbed wire on top. He took his jacket off, threw it over the barbs and scrambled over the fence. He could nip through the garden, out into the high street, down to the pub and away to safety.

 But there was no garden on the other side of the fence. Only a concrete-covered yard. The yard behind the shop, where, as it happened, Boss was waiting for him.

This was it. This was the moment Boss had lived for. A *Bad Man* was climbing into his yard. He was climbing over the fence backwards and there was his big, bad, burgling bottom, just waiting for Boss to sink his teeth into it.

Boss curled his lip and bared his enormous fangs. A growl began, deep in his belly, growing louder and fiercer, as his whole body shook with anticipation. With a terrifying howl, he launched himself toward the fence and the bad, bad man...

 Jenny had the Sunday paper spread out on the kitchen table.

'Top Dog in puppy farm scandal' blared the headline.

'I don't believe it!' she muttered as she read the report. It had been all over the TV too. Journalists had been busy and had uncovered many of Arlington's dirty secrets. His get-rich-quick schemes involved tricking people out of their money and his charitable work, supporting dog rescue homes, was a cover to find pedigree dogs to fill his puppy farms. He had three more farms in other parts of the country.

He was selling sick puppies for enormous prices, not caring about their health, and allowing the mothers to live in cruel, cramped conditions. The photographs were distressing. Jenny had tears in her eyes as she read on.

Walker's mum had been working hard at the council. They had found that Foxley Fields had been given to the village in 1862 by the lord of the manor at that time, and there was no way that anyone could claim to own it or the land that Jenny's house was built on.

Arlington was a chancer and a bully. He had learned that lies and fear would often make people give in to you, and his lawyer, Crispin Lightfoot, could make complicated lies look like the simple truth.

The newspaper thought Arlington would be going to prison for a long time.

'And good riddance too!' Jenny tapped the table and smiled. In the time that Walker had got to know her, it was the first time he had seen her really smile. She looked quite different. All the cares of the world had been lifted off her shoulders. Arlington had been ruining her life and now she was free of him. Walker was also happy to know that Thor and Loki were well and all the dogs at the puppy farm had been found new homes.

Walker stood up and put his cup and plate in

the sink. Jenny had made a particularly chocolatey sponge cake and Walker had eaten a particularly large slice of it. 'Time for a walk,' he said. 'But first I need to get Stella a new ball. Her old one is torn to shreds. I'll be back in a minute.'

 'Ah, Walker!' said Mr Bonus. 'Good to see you!'

Walker looked at Anje, who was sitting behind the counter. Anje raised her eyebrows. What was her dad up to?

'You know about dogs,' said Mr Bonus. 'What is matter with my Boss? He's not eating his food. He look sad.'

'Can I see him?' Walker asked.

'Sure! Anje, take him out the back to see Boss, will you?'

Anje slipped off her chair and nodded for Walker to follow. The back of the shop was piled high with boxes full of everything you could imagine. They squeezed through a narrow passage made of kitchen towels and washing-up liquid boxes.

Anje folded her arms and leaned against the doorway as Walker approached Boss, holding out a hand for the dog to sniff.

'Hello!' Walker said quietly. He turned his back to Anje so she couldn't see them talking to each other. 'You were a bit of a hero the other night!' Walker said.

'Hmmf,' Boss grunted. 'You wouldn't think so. I'm still stuck here all day long. What's the point? I'm so bored!'

Walker nodded and stroked Boss's long, black ears.

Anje led him back into the shop.

'He's bored and depressed,' said Walker. 'He was a hero the other night and nobody cares. You can't keep a dog locked up all day. He'll get so depressed that when a real burglar tries to break in, he won't be bothered to protect you.'

Mr Bonus sighed and threw his hands in the air. 'So what do I do?'

'He needs to get out and run about and get some exercise,' said Walker.

'Ha!' Mr Bonus laughed. 'You very good businessman. You want me to pay you to take Boss for a walk every day.'

Walker frowned. 'That's not what I meant at all. Anje can take him for a walk,' he said. 'It's good for your business to have a healthy guard dog.'

'Anje?' Mr Bonus looked surprised. 'Anje is tiny little thing. Boss is a big dog!'

'But Boss loves Anje,' Walker explained. 'He'd do anything for her. And I can teach her how to walk him on the lead and help him to behave himself when she takes him out.'

'But Anje is so young.' Mr Bonus put his arm around his little girl. 'She can't go out all on her own.'

'She won't be on her own!' Walker laughed. 'She'll have a famous, deadly guard dog to protect her.'

Mr Bonus was silenced. He could think of no more reasons to keep Anje in the shop forever, or Boss locked up all day. In fact, he was beginning to understand that there might be benefits to keeping Boss fighting fit!

'I still can't believe it!' Anje laughed. My dad has never let me go out on my own before. It's unreal!'

Boss thought it was unreal too, racing across Foxley Fields, feeling the wind in his ears and the freedom of a wide open space for the first time.

Mr Bonus had given them a new ball thrower. They weren't selling as fast as he'd hoped and he needed the space for a new brand of hot chocolate he was promoting.

Stella and Boss raced each other to catch the ball. Boss was a bit clumsy and had one or two bad manners, but what can you expect of a dog that has been locked up all his life?

Stella liked having a friend to play with, and so did Walker. Stella dropped the ball at Walker's feet and winked.

'We should do this again,' said Walker, hurling the ball high into the air.

Anje nodded, thoughtfully. 'Yeah,' she smiled. 'That would be good!'